To all the kind people I know – C.C.

For my friends and neighbours, with love x – C.J-I.

First American Edition 2021
Kane Miller, A Division of EDC Publishing

Text copyright © Caroline Crowe 2021
Illustrations copyright © Cally Johnson-Isaacs 2021
The moral rights of the author and illustrator have been asserted.
First published 2021 by Macmillan Children's Books,
an imprint of Pan Macmillan
The Smithson, 6 Briset Street, London EC1M 5NR

For information contact:
Kane Miller, A Division of EDC Publishing
5402 S 122nd E Ave, Tulsa, OK 74146
www.kanemiller.com
www.usbornebooksandmore.com

Library of Congress Control Number: 2020949019

Printed and bound in China
1 2 3 4 5 6 7 8 9 10

ISBN: 978-1-68464-275-5

Caroline Crowe Cally Johnson-Isaacs

How Do You make a Rainbow?

Kane Miller
A DIVISION OF EDC PUBLISHING

"It's raining and it's pouring. Everything is sad and gray.
I think the sky needs cheering up! I wish there was a way . . .

How do you make a rainbow? Is it painted on the sky?
Help me paint one, Grandad. I'm too small to reach that high."

"A rainbow isn't painted,"
Whispers Grandad with a grin.
"It's made from hope and kindness,
With some other things thrown in . . .

It's the love that binds our family,
Friends who help us make it through.
It's thinking about others,
And the joy that brings to you.

It's tulips to say thank you,

Jam on toast to start the day,

And putting all your heart
Into the things you do or say.

It's kicking leaves in autumn,

Sunsets when the day is done,

Pumpkins lighting darkness,

Being tigers just for fun.

It's the glow you feel inside you,
When you make somebody proud.

It's when something's just so silly
That you have to laugh out loud.

It's sand between your toes,
It's the first signs that it's spring,
The funny face you get,
From sucking sour lemon zing.

It's croaking frogs with frog spawn,
It's helping plant new trees,

Picking peas and runner beans,
And grass stains on your knees.

It's taking time to listen,
When the birds sing songs for you,
And knowing when you wake up,
Every day is fresh and new.

It's caring for our oceans,
Picnics under summer skies,

Frosty winter mornings,

Butterflies and blueberry pies.

It's ballerinas' tutus,
Dancing like you just don't care.

It's singing songs together,

Having fun with punk rock hair.

Think of things that make you happy,
All the kind people that you know,

Find the sunshine that's inside you,
And a rainbow starts to grow . . .

And then before you know it,
Arching through the clouds so high,

You'll see a burst of color,
Lighting up the gloomy sky."

Make Your Very Own Rainbow!

Think of things that make you happy,
All the kind people that you know,
Find the sunshine that's inside you,
And a rainbow starts to grow . . .

Use these next few pages to create your very own personal rainbow of the things you love, and that are important to you. You could write, draw, color, or even cut out and stick in photos! It can be anything at all that is special to you.

Red

It's tulips to say thank you,
Jam on toast to start the day . . .

Be sure to ask an adult for help if you are using scissors!

~ Maybe you have a special red sweater that makes you feel warm and cozy?

What are your favorite red things?

Orange

Pumpkins lighting darkness,
Being tigers just for fun . . .

Which orange things are special to you?

Yellow

It's the glow you feel inside you,
When you make somebody proud . . .

Perhaps you have some
yellow rain boots for
splashing in puddles, or a
favorite yellow cuddly toy?

What makes your heart feel sunny and yellow?

Green

Picking peas and runner beans,
And grass stains on your knees . . .

What is special to you that is green?

Have you ever helped in
the garden, or played in the park?

Blue

Frosty winter mornings,
Butterflies and blueberry pies . . .

Draw, write, or stick in your special blue things here.

Indigo

It's ballerinas' tutus,
Dancing like you just don't care . . .

Indigo is a deep
blue-purple color!

Can you think of anything indigo that makes you happy?

Violet

It's singing songs together,
Having fun with punk rock hair . . .

Violet is a lighter,
pinky-purple color!

And then before you know it,
Arching through the clouds so high,
You'll see a burst of color,
Lighting up the gloomy sky.

What are your favorite violet things?
Draw, write, or stick them in here.